First published in 1986 in German by
Verlag Heinrich Ellermann, München as
Der einsame Riese.

© 1986 Verlag Heinrich Ellermann, München

English translation © 1986, Silver Burdett Company, Morristown, New Jersey.

ISBN 0-382-09377-1
Library of Congress Catalog Card Number 86-42823

First published in the United States in 1986 by Silver Burdett Company, Morristown,
New Jersey.

Published simultaneously in Canada by GLC/Silver Burdett Publishers, Agincourt,
Ontario.

Printed in West Germany.

The Lonesome Giant

Written and illustrated by Sophie Brandes

English translation by Michele F. Marcks

Silver Burdett

Morristown, New Jersey • Agincourt, Ontario

Not very long ago on the Mountain of the Giants there lived a giant whose name was Tulan. He was the last of a powerful race of giants and he lived all alone in a wild mountain cave high above a dark valley.

Tulan was not happy. His lonely life high up on the mountain cliffs made him miserable. Every day he would try to think of things to do to keep from being bored. Sometimes he would sit in a mountain stream and flood the surrounding countryside. Other times he would throw boulders down from the top of the mountain into the valley. These destructive pranks amused Tulan and his loud laugh resounded throughout the land. No humans dared to venture onto the Mountain of the Giants because they were so afraid of the wild Tulan. Even the mountain animals took flight from him.

The small village of Wolkenstein was nestled at the foot of this mountain. The villagers were very afraid of Tulan and his pranks were making life rather difficult for them. Every four weeks when the moon was full they heard Tulan roar in his giant voice: "Give me something to eat and drink, you measly humans. I have the hunger of a giant, and if you don't give me enough to eat I will make life even more dreadful for you!"

The villagers of Wolkenstein had no other choice but to load a wagon with the food they had worked so hard to grow and bring it to Tulan. They became poorer and poorer and they began to spend all their time thinking of some way to get rid of this bothersome giant.

very evening the villagers gathered in the Golden Apple Cafe and discussed the problem. One evening the master carpenter suggested that they block the entrance to his cave.

The beekeeper disagreed. "We must drive him out with smoke," he said.

"We have to find something that will make him go away, but what?" asked the mayor in exasperation.

An idea suddenly occurred to the town crier and his eyes sparkled with excitement. "Giants have very sensitive hearing," he began. "Even though they make so much noise themselves, they find the loud noises made by others unbearable."

"But how can that solve our problem?" asked the pharmacist.

"You know my daughter Camelia, don't you?" the town crier asked with a sly laugh. "And probably you've also heard her sing?"

"Yes we have. She sings very loudly!" exclaimed the pharmacist.

"And shrilly!" the master carpenter added.

"Well then, pay attention. And listen to my idea," said the town crier with just a hint of pride in his voice. "I believe that Camelia can drive away Tulan with her singing. Why, she can even shatter glass!"

"Oh, we don't believe you!" the men cried.

The town crier invited them all to come with him and hear for themselves.

The villagers could hear Camelia's deafening singing even before they reached the town crier's house. When they arrived Camelia greeted them with a high "C" that shook the walls. After that she hit a high "D" that jangled the mirror and caused the mayor's tame raven to fly madly about the room in fright.

"And now the high 'E'!" begged the visitors.

"No, I can't allow that! Who will pay for the damage?" the town crier insisted.

"We will!" promised the visitors in unison.

Straining and standing on her tiptoes, Camelia managed to reach the loudest high "E" that any human had ever heard.

The note penetrated right through the listeners to their very marrow. The chandelier shattered, the mirror broke into a thousand little pieces, and every glass in the house splintered.

"Enough, enough, we can't stand anymore!" cried the men as they covered their ears with their hands.

Finally, Camelia stopped singing and the men informed her of their plan.

espite feeling a little bit afraid when she heard what she would have to do, Camelia agreed to go along with the plan. She was a very brave girl and also very curious about how Tulan looked.

When the next full moon arrived the villagers gathered everything possible to satisfy Tulan: a sack filled with porridge oats, a crate of potatoes, a basket of turnips, a pig, bread, several bottles of sweet wine, and last but not least, eighty fresh eggs. All of this food was finally loaded onto a huge wagon which stood ready for the trip up the mountain.

As soon as the moon was round and full in the night sky, a horrible voice boomed from the direction of the mountains. "Tulan is hungry, Tulan is thirsty! Bring me something to eat! I you don't bring me enough you will regret it!"

His horrible voice echoed over mountain and valley, far into the distance. The good people of Wolkenstein shivered and quaked in the village square. They wished the brave Camelia luck as she and the two strong young men who had volunteered to accompany her left on their journey up the rugged mountain with the wagon full of food.

It was not hard to find the path. The moon shone as brightly as the sun shines during the day, and the high oak trees and pines cast long shadows. The wagon was bumped and jostled and Camelia kept asking, "Are we there yet?"

But the wagon climbed higher and higher in the mountains. Soon the tall trees were no longer visible. Only brushwood and rocks could survive at such a high altitude.

Finally they reached their destination and the wagon came to a halt. Camelia's two young companions jumped from the wagon, and before she could stop them they had disappeared.

It was so still that Camelia believed she could hear everything around her shivering in the cold. "Oh, if only I was safe at home in my nice warm bed," she thought. But finally she collected her courage and yelled so loudly that her voice echoed off the cliffs, "Tulan! Can you hear me? I have brought you food and drink!"

Soon afterwards a voice bellowed back from the cliffs. "Wait. I will come and take what I need."

There was a great rumbling and crashing, as if a lion was making its way through the brush. Then the mighty giant suddenly appeared in front of Camelia. Twelve giant steps — and the horrible Tulan stood so close to her she could see the evil glint in his eye.

His mighty figure towered against the starry sky. His beard, adorned with ice crystals, glittered in the moonlight.

"Where is my food?" he roared.

Tulan began to get angry, but Camelia stopped him by singing a song so loud that he lost his sight and his hearing. He clamped his hands over his ears to stop the pain. Then, full of wonder, he contemplated the singer.

"What kind of wonderful creature are you?" he asked. "I have never before seen anyone so graceful and beautiful."

Tulan was so enchanted with Camelia that his heart began to ache.

"What is your name, wonderful creature?" he whispered.

"I am Camelia the singer."

"Oh, please stay with me!" he begged. "I am a lonely giant, but if I had you here with me I would be happy."

"Is that what you think?" retorted Camelia. "I should stay here with a stupid old giant like you? Everything that you have is too big for me: your feet, your hands, your mouth, and especially your stomach!"

"But what could I do so you will like me?" Tulan whined.

The crafty Camelia thought a minute and replied, "Eat less and shrink!"

Then she turned around, called to her drivers, and started back down the mountain.

Tulan stayed behind where Camelia had left him and cried over his broken heart. Oh, he was so lonely and so much in love!

s morning came Camelia finally reached the town. Once the wagon arrived at the marketplace all sorts of people ran over to her. They were very curious and anxious to know what had happened.

The people asked so many questions she didn't know where to begin.

"Did you sing to him?" the town crier wanted to know.

"What did he look like?" the beekeeper wanted to know.

"Did you see his cave?" questioned the master carpenter.

"Did you manage to drive him away?" all of the villagers demanded in unison.

"Where did you hear all of that?" Camelia laughingly asked "Who told you such ghastly tales?"

And she went on her way and burst into song. Nevertheless the villagers were satisfied and they praised the courageous Camelia. And no one said anything as here and there a street lamp or a windowpane shattered as Camelia sang her loudest and shrillest.

The days went by and as the full moon approached the villagers wondered whether Camelia would visit Tulan again on the Mountain of the Giants.

One evening when the moon was almost full the people of Wolkenstein heard a familiar voice, but the voice was soft and far away and barely audible in the village.

"Tulan is hungry and thirsty. Come, bring me something to eat and drink!"

The villagers groaned and dragged together what they could find to feed Tulan. The next morning Camelia harnessed the horses and had the wagon loaded with food. She took the two strong young men along again for protection.

The moon shone brightly as they drove through the dark valley but this time Camelia knew the way.

"Tulan, I am here!" she called as she reached her destination. "I have brought the food that you demanded!"

Camelia looked around herself and was amazed because the wilderness had undergone such a great change. Where there were once rocks and underbrush now plowed fields spread out in all directions. In one field giant turnips were growing. Fences enclosed the fields, and even the plug of ice at the mouth of Tulan's cave had melted. Just as Camelia became impatient from waiting the giant leaped down the slope to her.

Even though Tulan still appeared powerful it seemed that he had somehow changed since the last full moon.

"My lovely Camelia," he said, "you have finally come to stay with me."

"That's what you think!" she retorted. "I have only come to squelch your insatiable hunger!" And she began to unload the wagon.

"idn't I do what you told me to do?" whined Tulan.

"I have fasted and worked until I was too tired to move. I built a fence, tilled a field, and dug a well. And look at me! Aren't I already much thinner and smaller? Say something, my dearest Camelia!"

"All that you have said is quite true," answered the cunning Camelia. "As far as I can tell anyway in this gloomy light. But you are still too enormous for me. Your beard is too thick, your eyes too wild, your handshake too vigorous, and the path to your cave too tiring!"

Meanwhile, the wagon was unloaded. The giant looked sadly at Camelia.

"It is too difficult to be alone." Tulan moaned. "What do I have to do so you will stay with me?"

Camelia composed herself and said, apparently undisturbed "Very simple! Continue to fast, abstain from drinking wine, go to sleep early, be self-reliant, watch over your herd, build stairs and put windows in your cave."

Poor Tulan, standing there with his giant turnips, began to shed giant tears.

"Farewell," said Camelia. "I will return in a month to see how you are getting along."

Camelia broke Tulan's heart because she would not stay. She climbed aboard the wagon and hurriedly started back to the village.

When she returned she was again bombarded with questions about Tulan the Giant. Was he angry and vengeful? Had Camelia driven him away? But the brave Camelia just shrugged her shoulders, laughed, and remained silent.

The villagers of Wolkenstein were satisfied because they had been spared Tulan's wrath.

Camelia continued to sing, but her tone too grew softer and sweeter.

"It seems to me that my daughter has somehow been trans-formed," declared the town crier to his circle of friends. "I wish I knew her secret."

The days passed. The moon disappeared and then came back. Soon it was full again, but everything was quiet and still on the Mountain of the Giants. Nothing stirred. The people of Wolkenstein said to each other: "It appears to be true. Tulan has disappeared! Camelia has driven him away with her singing. Long live Camelia!"

And they celebrated with a grand festival around the well in the center of the marketplace. Unknown to the celebrating villagers, Camelia had secretly and quietly slipped away at the crack of dawn.

"A promise is a promise," she said to herself as she climbed on a mule.

uring the long and tiring ride through the lonely valley fog crowded in around her. There were several times when Camelia was afraid that she had lost her way. But then suddenly, with the singing of the birds, the fog disappeared. Morning had finally arrived. Camelia had to go the rest of the way on foot because the mule refused to move.

"Tulan!" she called into the dawn. "Are you there?"

Nothing moved. When Camelia looked around she saw a plowed field full of winter wheat and a beautifully walled well. Sheep and goats were standing around it, drinking peacefully. Then she saw the stairs, many hundred steps high. Camelia imagined how Tulan had sweated and toiled to build them, and her heart softened. She climbed up the steps. At the top was a wonderful view of the valley, and of the streams, forests, and fields all the way down to the village of Wolkenstein.

Camelia finally came to a house built into the cliffs. It looked much different than the giant's cave had looked. It had two windows with wonderful blue panes of glass and a door that was intricately carved. The roof was supported by two stone pillars. Mountain grass and the most beautiful flowers grew on top of it. Three baby mountain goats were grazing there.

Camelia knocked timidly.

A man's voice, neither loud nor soft, answered, "Sing me a song and you may come in!"

Camelia sang the music that was in her head and entered the house. She found a very friendly looking man sitting at a table in the center of the room. A flock of lambs was gathered around him.

"Come, have some breakfast with me," he said.

So they shared bread and goat cheese, milk and jam.

"Why are you looking at me like that?" he asked.

"I cannot believe that you are really the terrible Tulan," Camelia replied. "Your face is not rough, your stomach is not fat, your hands are gentle with the animals, and your eyes are kind and twinkling like the morning star." She laughed. "Only your beard hasn't changed!" Then Cameli became serious. "Why have you stopped calling to us?"

"And why, in spite of all that, have you still come her to visit me?"

"So that I could see you again," she said.

"And what do you see?" asked Tulan.

"I see Tulan, the man I love."

Then Tulan, who was a giant no longer, went to Cameli and they stood for a long time, arm in arm, looking into eac other's eyes.

Camelia never did return to Wolkenstein. She stayed in th mountains with Tulan, married him, and helped him look afte his flock of lambs and herd of goats. She sang soft songs to thei children. They grew old together, and lived happily ever afte on the Mountain of the Giants.